Whispers to the Gods

Essays and Poetry

Midnightzky

Ukiyoto Publishing

All global publishing rights are held by

Ukiyoto Publishing

Published in 2025

Content Copyright © Midnightzky
ISBN 9789370098091

All rights reserved.

No part of this publication may be reproduced, transmitted, or stored in a retrieval system, in any form by any means, electronic, mechanical, photocopying, recording or otherwise, without the prior permission of the publisher.

The moral rights of the author have been asserted.

This is a work of fiction. Names, characters, businesses, places, events, locales, and incidents are either the products of the author's imagination or used in a fictitious manner. Any resemblance to actual persons, living or dead, or actual events is purely coincidental.

This book is sold subject to the condition that it shall not by way of trade or otherwise, be lent, resold, hired out or otherwise circulated, without the publisher's prior consent, in any form of binding or cover other than that in which it is published.

www.ukiyoto.com

Dedication

This work is dedicated to the beautiful souls who have shaped my journey and fueled my words. To my friends—Mica, Racheille, LJ, and Primacell—your unwavering support has been the steady ground beneath my dreams, reminding me that even the quietest beginnings can lead to something extraordinary. To the dreamers who inspire me—Paj, Natalie, Jushly, Aiah, Darleanne, Ash, Vernice, and Shin—your encouragement breathes life into every page I create. To my family, whose love has been my strongest foundation, thank you for believing in every story I dared to tell. To my cousin, Ate Romela, who first opened the door to the world of writing and taught me that stories are worth chasing. And to Ukiyuto Publishing, for giving me the chance to turn my words into something real and let my work find a home beyond my heart.

Contents

Chapter 1	1
Devotion to the Torn Skies	1
Chapter 2	5
Crowned in Betrayal	5
Chapter 3	9
Tides of Vengeance: A Heart Left to Sink	9
Chapter 4	12
Beneath the River Lethe	12
Chapter 5	14
Through the Seasons of Nurturing Love	14
Chapter 6	17
The Great Shield of Fiercest Hearts	17
Chapter 7	20
A Brilliant Harmony of Romance	20
Chapter 8	23
Under the Gentle Moonlight	23
Chapter 9	26
Warrior of the Heart: To Fight Within	26
Chapter: 10	29
Tempting Hearts: Desire of the Desired	29
Chapter 11	32
Forged In Love, Steeled by Trust	32
Chapter 12	35
The Messenger's Heart	35

Chapter 13	38
Intoxicated	38
Chapter 14	40
In the Quiet Hearth: The Heart Moves On	40
Chapter 15	42
To Rise From the Depths	42
About the Author	45

Chapter 1
Devotion to the Torn Skies

Love is not the gentle murmur of the breeze nor the soft kiss of the rain; it is the mighty rumble of thunder shaking the earth and the blinding flash of lightning rending the very heavens. Love arrives as a tempest—untamed, wild, and without invitation. It will not be subdued or controlled. It demands to be felt, in all its overwhelming power, in all its exquisite ruin. One cannot reason with it, nor predict it. One may only stand, heart quaking, and surrender to its fierce embrace.

The ancients, those sages of yore, perceived the truth that the heavens reveal. The Greeks, with their profound insight, believed that when the sky was torn asunder by lightning, it was Zeus himself, in all his majesty, hurling his fury from the summit of Olympus. Each clap of thunder was his divine utterance, a pronouncement of his omnipotent power. To dread the storm was to dread the god. Yet, they also knew that to stand in awe of it, to behold its unrestrained grandeur even as it threatened annihilation, was to honor the divine. In their dread, they discovered something sacred—and in that sacred terror, a love more profound than mortal hearts could ever fathom.

This, then, is how I view love—not as a gentle and secure thing, but as something vast, something terrifying, capable of both tender grace and crushing destruction. Love builds, and love burns; it blesses, and it curses. It does not arrive to offer comfort. It arrives to demand surrender. And within that surrender, amid the fear and trembling, love teaches us reverence. It asks us to lift our eyes to the darkened sky, to smile even as the thunder shakes the ground beneath our feet.

Love, like Zeus, commands everything. It tears down the walls we erect around our hearts and fills the corners of our lives with the light of divine fire. It offers no mercy to the timid heart. And yet, in its cruelty, there is a strange, paradoxical mercy—the mercy of being truly alive, of feeling something far greater than oneself. Love does not promise safety; it promises only transformation.

So, my dearest, if ever you find yourself wondering what love truly is, remember this: *it is the storm*, and it is the god who rules it. It is fire in the sky, and thunder in the soul. It is standing beneath the fury of it all—drenched, trembling, blinded by light—and still lifting your face to the heavens, whispering, I would choose this again.

In its violence, love carries an unexpected mercy—the mercy of experiencing life fully, of being swept away by something far beyond our control. To love is not to remain untouched, but to be transformed by something immense, something powerful. Love, like Zeus, does not promise peace; it promises the strength to endure its storms.

How can one feel such trembling and not offer up a prayer to the god of storms himself?

Thus, with my heart laid bare beneath the fury of his skies, I cry:

O Zeus, All-Father,

Lord of the Thundercloud,

King whose voice rends the heavens and shatters the bones of the earth,

hear the cry of thy child.

I stand upon the shattered stones,

beneath the tempestuous heavens thou hast wrought with thy mighty hand.

I stand where the winds tear the voice from my throat,

and still, I call thy name.

Hurl thy lightning, O Thunderer!

Let it strike the fear from my heart, the weakness from my limbs.

Baptize me not with gentle rain, but with fire from the heavens,

that I may know the purity of love untamed.

O Zeus, God King!

teach me to love as thou lovest—

fierce and immortal, unbowed by fear, unbroken by doubt.

Let my heart be as thy storm: wild, holy, and everlasting.

Grant me not peace, but passion.

Grant me not silence, but the roaring song of life.
Carve thy will into my soul with the sharp edge of thy lightning bolt,
and I shall wear thy mark proudly among mortals.

O King of Immortals,
whose gaze sets mountains aflame and oceans trembling,
breathe into me thy sacred fire.
Make me bold, make me strong, make me worthy of the storm.

For to love is to worship,
and to worship is to burn,
and to burn is to be made eternal.

By thunder, by flame, by breath of sky,
I am thine.

Chapter 2
Crowned in Betrayal

I never imagined that romance could be such a deceiver. Love, I once believed, was a pure and unbreakable thing. Yet, how easily it betrays, not with the fierce crash of storms, but with the slow, insidious decay of broken promises. I once held it sacred, a union to be cherished, but now I see how swiftly it fractures, how even the sweetest vows can turn bitter. And in my grief, my mind turns to you, Hera—Queen of Heaven, crowned in gold and revered by a thousand cities. I find myself pitying you, for you too were loved in name, but wounded in truth.

You, most mighty of all, who ruled beside Zeus and wore your title like a crown of jewels, were yet betrayed again and again. Your wrath, I now see, was not the result of pettiness, but of the deepest of heartaches—the sort of betrayal that mocks even a goddess's worth. They called you jealous, but I now behold you through a different view. I pity the rage that burned within you, the bitterness that took root, not because you were weak, but because you remained faithful to one who could not honor you in return. I understand you now, though I wish I had never had to.

They call you jealous. I call you indomitable. You, crowned in gold and honored by mortals and immortals alike, were still betrayed. Yet you did not break. You did not crumble into dust. You did not vanish into sorrow. Rather, you sharpened your fury into a weapon. You made your throne from the shattered promises of those who wronged you. Your jealousy was not cruelty—it was simply grief, armored and unyielding. You taught me that jealousy is not always the mark of cruelty—it is sometimes the armor of grief. You showed me that even goddesses bleed when wronged. No crown, no matter how splendid, can shield the heart from breaking. If you, Queen of Heaven, could be betrayed and yet still rise, shining brighter than all Olympus, then perhaps there is hope for me as well. Perhaps my heartbreak does not diminish me, but rather reforges me into something stronger, something fiercer.

So here I stand, my heart shattered and my pride bruised, lifting my eyes to you, Hera. I do not seek to have him returned to me. I do not ask for the restoration of what has been lost. I only seek the strength you bore—strength to walk away while my crown still held high, strength to transform betrayal into fire, strength to burn with righteous anger without letting it consume me.

Oh Queen, most noble and most wronged, teach me to be royal even amid betrayal. Teach me to make of my heartbreak a coronation, of my sorrow a scepter.

Make me relentless. Make me sacred. Make me, like you, unforgettable.

And so I pray:

O Hera, Queen of Heaven,
Golden-crowned Lady of High Olympus,

Bride betrayed, heart unconquered,
Hear my voice from thy lofty throne of pride and tempest.

I have known thy fury; I have worn thy sorrow as a raiment.
I have tasted the bitterness thou drinkest from thy jewelled cup.

O Lady of Sacred Bonds,
Thou who hast watched thy beloved stray,
Thou who hast borne each wound and yet risen, resplendent,
Impart to me the sacred art of surviving betrayal.

They call thee jealous—I call thee faithful.
They name thee wrathful—I call thee wounded.
They scorn thy anger—but I revere it,
For anger is the armour forged by the brokenhearted.

O Hera, stronger than forgiveness itself,
Teach me to wield my rage as a sceptre,
To weave my sorrow into a robe befitting a queen.

Teach me to love myself with a constancy he could not offer.
Teach me to be fierce, not fragile;
Sacred, not shattered.

Let my diadem never slip, even though my heart bleeds.
Let my laughter outsing the echoes of my weeping.
Let my pride stand brighter than the ruins he left behind.

O Consort of the Thunderer, Sovereign of Oaths,
Look upon me with thine eyes sharp as blades and brilliant as stars.
Bless me with a love for myself, unbreakable,
That no betrayal shall ever again profane.

Make me royal once more.
Make me invincible once more.
Make me crowned — even amidst the ruins of love.

Chapter 3
Tides of Vengeance: A Heart Left to Sink

I shall submerge him in the depths of the ocean until he forgets the very taste of air. I will drag him beneath the waves, where his lungs will be shattered by the silence he once imposed upon me. I will flood his soul with the salt of the sea, the same salt that he so callously sewed into mine, each wound a surge that I shall now release upon him.

Poseidon, Lord of the Endless Deep, Earthshaker, Master of Tides and Tempests, hear my plea. Bless these hands that once reached for love, now clasped only in the cold embrace of vengeance. Bless this heart, once devoted to him, now a vessel only for rage, filled with the relentless surge of a tidal wave.

Let the tide of my fury rise within me, cold and merciless as the darkest ocean. Let my love become a burden that he cannot carry, a weight heavier than the very oceans that crash upon the shore. Let my name, uttered in the final moments of his despair, be the last sound he ever breathes before the sea claims him as its own.

I will offer you everything just to become the great wave that crashes against the jagged rocks of his deceit, the undertow that pulls him ever deeper into the abyss. Let the vast, unfathomable depths of my sorrow consume him, until no light remains to guide your way.

I will offer my very soul to become the foam of the tempest, the wreckage of shattered ships. I will be marked by the fury of storms, the wrath of Poseidon himself. I will be the tide that never retreats, the current that sweeps away all that dares to stand in its path.

Let him drown in the love he thought he could betray. Let him drown in me, as the ocean swallows all that dares to defy its will.

I beg you, Poseidon, I beg you to hear my prayer:

O Lord of the Endless Deep,
Master of Tides, Earthshaker, Lord of the Waters,
Hear the cry of my heart, rising like the storm-tossed sea.

I offer everything I have left — my heart, my soul, my brokenness —

To the fury of your oceans.
In the fathomless blackness of your depths,
I seek the strength to avenge the love you ripped from me.

Make me the crashing wave,
The tempest that knows no mercy.
Let my fury surge with the tide,
My sorrow as boundless as the fathomless sea.

Make me the wave that crashes with fury,

The tempest that will not relent,
Let my rage rise with the tide,
My sorrow endless as the ocean itself.

O Poseidon, Breaker of Oaths,
I beg you to grant me the storm,
To wash away the lies that have torn me apart.
Let him drown in the love he dared betray,
Let him be consumed by the very depths of his own treachery.

Chapter 4
Beneath the River Lethe

I will bury myself in the darkness you command. I will lay down my heart, torn and useless, at your feet. Without her, there is no point in stepping through this life. Without her, the world is colorless, weightless, empty.

Oh Hades, Lord of the Silent Lands, Keeper of Lost Souls, hear me. Take me into your cold kingdom. Shelter me in the silence where no memories follow, where no false hope lingers. Let me vanish in the place where broken things are allowed to rest.

I do not come here by fate's heavy hands. I come by the weight of my own grief. I drag myself willingly into the dark, because living without her is no different from dying a thousand deaths each day. I do not fear your shadows. I fear the light that reminds me of what I lost.

Let the river Lethe wash from my lips the sacred name she once held. Let it extinguish the very echoes of her voice that cling so desperately to my soul. Let me sleep in the dark soil of thy kingdom, where sorrow itself dare not tread, where even grief forgets to weep.

I do not pray for rescue. I do not pray for reunion. I pray only for silence — for the blessed stillness where her memory cannot haunt me. I pray to sink so deep that not even the gods can call me back.

Embrace me with the dust of abandoned dreams. Mark me with the stillness of a heart that has nothing left to give. Make me a shadow, a ghost among your endless halls, a soul that chose oblivion when love chose to leave.

I gave her every inch of my soul. And now, I give to you the remnants of a spirit too broken to endure the pain of existence any longer.

I am begging you, my Lord.

God of the Underworld, hear my prayer,

for my heart has known the weight of grief.

Take this broken soul and make it whole,

for without her, life is a shadow, an empty shell.

Grant me rest from the pain of love unreturned,

grant me peace in the silence where her memory fades.

Let me lay down my burdens at Your feet,

and in Your mercy, may I find the strength to forgive myself.

I do not ask for joy, nor for love to return,

but for release from this endless ache.

Lift me from this darkness,

and guide me to the stillness where I may rest in Your grace.

For I am weary, Pluton,

and my heart has given all it could give.

Take what remains, and heal it with Your peace.

Chapter 5
Through the Seasons
of Nurturing Love

I am, by nature, generous enough to bestow the fullness of my love without condition, and gentle enough to offer my heart with a smile of unguarded tenderness. Yet never again shall I permit my love to be seized as spoil, leaving behind barren wastelands where once I sowed gardens of devotion.

It was I who scattered seeds with bare and willing hands, trusting in the sacred hope that beauty and faithfulness would rise from the tilled earth of my soul. It was I who opened my heart as fertile ground, that others might find rest and abundance within my warmth. My spirit was once a field of wild and golden plenty — not some desolate land to be ravaged by careless and covetous hands.

To those who mistook the breadth of my love for frailty, to those who uprooted my trust and set fire to the fields I so tenderly nurtured, know this: *the season of famine is come.* No longer shall I squander the harvest of my heart upon those who would trample it beneath ungrateful feet.

Thus do I turn now to thee, Oh Demeter — Bearer of the Sickle, Mother of the Verdant Earth, Mistress of the Sacred Cycle. Thou whose sorrow made the world itself wither, and whose fury compelled even the proudest of gods to kneel before the barren fields —

teach me to guard well the soil of my heart. Teach me to withhold my rain, to summon drought and desolation against those who approach me with hands empty of reverence and hearts barren of loyalty.

My gardens shall yet flourish, but never again shall they yield their fruits to the faithless. My wheat shall rise still toward the heavens, but thorns and tempests shall now stand sentinel about it. I shall yet offer life — but I shall know, too, the solemn hour in which it is meet to summon the long winter and let the earth fall silent.

Let my roots twine deeper into the secret heart of the earth, unseen and unbroken. Let my vines thicken and my thorns sharpen into daggers against the greedy. Let my love be a harvest that nourishes those who honor it — and leaves the betrayers starving in their thirst.

They may tear at my flowers. They may scorch the bright meadows of my spirit. They may believe they have laid waste to all I gave. Yet never shall they touch the sacred seed of love buried deep within me — a seed that no betrayal can wither, nor grief uproot.

I am both the soil and the sickle.

The blessing and the famine.

The field that blooms in love — and the field that burns in loss.

And never again shall my love be plundered.

Thus now, in the waning light, I lift my voice unto thee:

O Demeter, Mother of Grain and Grief,
Goddess of Sacred Soil and Silent Fury,
hear me.

I who have planted and planted,
I who have watered with open hands,
now call to thee in sorrow and in strength.

Teach me to guard the seeds of my spirit.
Teach me when to open the fields in trust,
and when to call forth the long famine in vengeance.

Let my roots sink deep where no thief may reach.
Let my rains fall only upon worthy soil.
Let my sickle be sharpened against those who come
with barren hearts and grasping hands.

Mark me with thy golden crown of wheat.
Strengthen me with the stones of the enduring earth.
Let my harvest be fierce,
my love be wild,
and my spirit remain ever untaken —
as sacred as the first fields thou didst ever sow.

Chapter 6
The Great Shield of Fiercest Hearts

I have come to understand that love is not a mere contest, nor a struggle in which I am destined to falter. It is a war I enter not in desperation, but in conviction, armed with the wisdom to protect what is precious, and the courage to defend it with every fiber of my being. My heart, encased in the armor of reason, is not something to be begged for or won by force, but something to be cherished and safeguarded.

I do not kneel for affection, for it is not in the act of submission that I find strength. Rather, I stand tall, resolute, offering my love to those worthy of its light, and guarding it fiercely against those who would seek to claim it without regard. I am the warrior who bears in one hand the olive branch of peace, and in the other, the spear of fierce protection. I offer peace to the deserving, yet I stand unflinching in battle when my honor or my heart is threatened.

It is to you, Athena, I turn — Goddess of Wisdom and War, Lady of the Unbroken Mind and the Sharpened Blade. You, who crafted empires from thought and led with both wisdom and unyielding strength, who stood untouchable and undefeated in the face of all adversity. Teach me to wield love with the sharpness of your blade, as a shield that defends rather than a chain that binds. Teach me to choose my battles wisely and to walk away from those unworthy of my strength.

I do not lower my sword for those who do not see my worth. I do not waste my strategy on those who cannot meet me with equal resolve. I am unshaken, a fortress built from both stone and spirit, enduring through all storms. Let those who seek my love do so with hearts steadfast and strong, for I will not give it away lightly. My love is not a kingdom for the unworthy, but a treasure to be shielded by the fiercest of hearts.

Now, I pray:

Oh Athena, Goddess of Wisdom and Courage,
Guardian of the Aegis,
hear my plea.

Grant me the sight of the owl,
that I may see the truth in all things.
Sharpen my mind like your sacred blade,
that I may walk through love with the strength of conviction.

Let my heart be a shield of courage,
strong and steadfast in its defense.
Let my soul be an invincible fortress,
and my love, a treasure — guarded but never withheld.

Bless me with the wisdom to build,
the strength to protect,
and the courage to love without losing myself.

Oh Daughter of Zeus,
make me a warrior of my own heart,
worthy of my own kingdom.

Chapter 7
A Brilliant Harmony of Romance

Love came to me as gently as the first rays of dawn, a soft and warming light that awakened my soul from its long, shadowed slumber. It was the quiet, delicate melody of a song I had never known I needed, yet in an instant, the world seemed to dance in perfect harmony.

This love was no cacophony of forceful sounds or overwhelming gestures. Rather, it was a symphony of light, tender and soothing, like the warmth of the sun filtering through the leaves of an ancient tree, or the subtle embrace of a morning breeze. It was unlike anything I had ever known before—like a flame that melted the cold, hardened heart I had so long protected. A fire that did not scorch, but glowed, like the sun itself rising for me alone.

Yet with this newfound warmth comes a question that lingers in my mind: How can I keep it? How can I preserve the brilliance of this love—the sunlight—when the world about me seems so often draped in shadow?

I turn now to thee, Apollo—God of the Sun, Illuminator of the Dark, and the Music that Guides the Soul. Thou who carriest the sun in thy hands, who guideth thy chariot across the firmament, banishing the night and heralding the day. Thou, whose light illuminates the world in all its grandeur. How can I remain, like thee, bright and warm, even when all around me is cold, and uncertainty reigns?

I long to cherish this love forever, Apollo. I wish to hold it as I would the sun in the palm of my hand, never letting it fade, never permitting it to be swallowed by the encroaching shadows.

Let my heart be as a melody, a song that never ceases, a tune that fills the silence with its comforting warmth. Let my love remain as radiant as the sun itself, enduring and unyielding.

Now, I wish for you to hear my plea:

Apollo, Lord of Light and Music,
Bearer of the Sun's Eternal Warmth,
Hear me.

Grant that I may carry thy light within me,
To shine without ever fading.
Let me be the melody that soothes the soul,
The warmth that never leaves.

Guide me, as thou guidest the day,
To cherish this love as thou dost cherish the dawn
Gentle, brilliant, and ever shining.

Bestow upon me the wisdom to preserve its brilliance,
To hold it without fear,
And to love with a spirit unbroken.
May my heart sing as thou dost in the heavens,
And my soul glow with the golden rays thou dost bring.

Chapter 8
Under the Gentle Moonlight

Oh Artemis, Lady of the Silver Bow, Huntress of the Wilds, and Queen of the Moon's Light, I beseech thee to guide me as I hunt for love. I have never known it as others have—no passionate fire, no overwhelming blaze, no tempest that consumes. For me, love has always been like the moon—gentle, serene, and distant. It has never burned brightly in my life but has instead shone with a soft, pale glow from afar, like the tranquil light reflected upon still waters in the quiet hours of the night. It beckons to me, yet remains ever beyond my grasp.

I have not known love to be a force that sweeps me away, nor a consuming light. Yet I feel its quiet pull, persistent and steady, like the waxing and waning of the moon itself. It is a mystery that I yearn to comprehend. I have watched it from the shadows, witnessed its dance in the hearts of others, yet I have never dared to step into its light. I wish to pursue it, to learn its rhythm, to approach it with the same care and grace with which you tread upon the forest's floor, silent and strong.

Oh Artemis, Protector of the Wilds, Mistress of the Forests, and Daughter of Zeus, I seek thy guidance. Teach me how to track love as you would your prey. Let me approach it with patience, as one would approach a creature in the wild—with gentleness and careful observation. I shall not chase it recklessly. No,

I shall wait for the right moment, the right sign, and when love reveals itself, I shall know how to approach it, as you know how to strike when the time is right.

I do not seek a love that burns with great intensity, only to fade as swiftly as it ignited. I seek a love that is constant, like the moon in the sky—steady, unwavering, and eternal. A love that may grow with time, a love that I may come to understand and cherish. I desire to hold it gently, as one would cradle the moonlight—not in force, but with reverence and respect.

And so, I pray:

Oh Artemis, Lady of the Silver Bow,
Protector of the Wilds, and Mistress of the Forests,
Guide me through the darkened sky,
Help me track love with patience and insight,
Like the moon that watches from on high.

I shall not rush nor seek with haste,
But wait for love at my own pace.
Like thee, I shall remain calm and still,
Guided by patience, strength, and will.

Let me hunt love with quiet grace,
Not with fear, but in thy embrace.

Teach me to see its quiet glow,
And cherish it, as stars do below.

Oh Artemis, Lady beloved of all,
Goddess of the Moon's Light,
With thy light, help me to understand why
Love, like prey, must be sought with care,
And in time, its beauty shall be there.

Chapter 9
Warrior of the Heart: To Fight Within

Love is no gentle thing. It is a battlefield, and I shall march into its fray as a warrior— clad in armour, resolute, and ready to shed blood if such be the cost to claim it. I have gazed upon love from afar, but now, I have come to understand its true price. It is not a pursuit for the faint-hearted. It demands everything. It calls for sacrifice, for strength, for courage. Love, indeed, is war, and I shall fight for it with all that I am.

In this great battle, I shall not flinch. I shall not falter. I will advance, sword drawn, ready to meet the chaos head-on. For love is no place of peace and tranquillity; it is a place of strife, of unanticipated trials, of rising tensions. Those who seek it must be prepared for the inevitable clash of wills, the storms that will assail them, and the sacrifices they must make. This is not a struggle for the weak nor the timid; it is a battle that will test the very core of one's being — *heart, strength, and soul.*

I shall shed blood for love, for it is a prize worth such a cost. I know that in order to hold it, to possess it wholly, I must prove myself worthy. I must show that I fear not the sacrifices it demands, that I can endure all that the war of love brings. It is not the battle itself that matters, but the reward that lies beyond it: the victory of holding love in my hands, the glory of knowing that I fought for it with every fibre of my being.

I turn now to thee, O Ares, God of War, for thy esteemed guidance. Thou who hast fought in countless battles, who understandeth the true price of victory, teach me to harness this fierce energy within me. Help me to rise when all else falters, to remain unyielding in the face of love's cruelest trials. Guide me in this combat, for I shall not surrender, not until love is mine to claim.

Love, indeed, is war, and I shall fight until the very end. I shall bleed for it. I shall face every challenge, unflinching, without hesitation. For love, in all its splendour and agony, is a battlefield worth conquering.

Now, I pray unto thee:

Lord Ares, God of War,
Wielder of the Mighty Spear,
Grant unto me the strength to battle for love.
Let my heart become a battlefield,
Where passion and fear doth clash.

Guide my sword when the conflict rages,
And raise my shield when love threateneth to fall.
Let my blood be spilled if it must,
For love is the war I shall win.

Teach me to charge forward,
Without faltering, without retreat.
Let no enemy of love stand in mine way,
For I shall fight, and I shall conquer,
Until victory is mine.

Chapter: 10
Tempting Hearts: Desire of the Desired

I have ever been the one who captures hearts with but a smile, with a mere glance, and with the graceful sway of my form. Men fall before me with a single word, with but the lightest touch, and I, without reluctance, allow them to do so. I have wandered through their affections, played among their fleeting emotions, and offered them dreams they were all too eager to believe. Yet none have loved the woman who hides behind the beauty, the one whose soul aches for something more.

They are drawn to my allure and the exterior that adorns me, yet none possess the insight to perceive the longing which lies beneath my laughter, the yearning for a love genuine and true. It is simple to be a temptress and bask in their fleeting desires, but it is far more difficult to find a love that is not but a passing infatuation. I have stolen hearts without effort, yet I seek one that will endure, one that will see me in my entirety, beyond the surface, and beyond the transient beauty.

I am Aphrodite's daughter, born of beauty and desire, but I weary of being naught but a fleeting dream. I seek a love not based upon a glance or a mere touch, but upon something far deeper— something that transcends the physical and touches the very essence of who I am. I long for a love not built upon my looks, nor upon the charm I possess, but upon a connection that neither time nor circumstance can sever.

Aphrodite, Queen of Desire — though I may not possess thy divine hand, I share thy endless hunger for a love that endures.

Guide me toward a love that does not flicker like a candle in the wind — a love that stands unmoved through storm and silence alike. Teach me to guard my heart even as I give it. Teach me to discern the love that sees me whole, beyond the blinding sight of what I appear to be.

And so, to thee, I offer my sweetest prayer:

Lovely Aphrodite, Goddess of Grace,
Let my beauty light every shadowed place.
Like the rose I bear — tender yet bold,
Let my story of love be worth being told.

With dove's wings, let my spirit soar,
In passion's light, forevermore.
Lead me to a love that will not stray,
One that endures, come break or day.

Let my seashell sing a song of truth,
Of a love untouched by fading youth.

Not merely for beauty, nor fleeting fire,
But for a soul that love shall never tire.

Show me a heart that sees me through,
One who will cherish the spirit I grew.
Guide me to the one who dares believe,
Not just in what I seem — but in all I am, and all I dream.

Chapter 11
Forged In Love, Steeled by Trust

I do not bear my heart upon my sleeve, for such finery is unfit for the truth of love. Rather, I bear it as one would bear a suit of armour — wrought by fire, beaten by sorrow, tempered by solitude. I seek not the honeyed phrases of idle courtship nor the delicate promises that falter with the dawn. I do not speak of love with the softness that others so dearly crave. Instead, I forge it— slowly, steadily— with hands that have built kingdoms and raised walls: walls high enough to keep the world at bay, and strong enough to shield the few I dare to let within.

They call me cold and stoic. They misinterpret my silence as indifference. Yet they do not comprehend that true love is not found in clamor and haste— it is forged, like the finest blade within the fiercest fire. It is not seized in moments of fleeting passion; it is built over time, wrought by trust and by unwavering purpose. I shall not fall for those who falter in the face of such heat.

I have known the treachery that leaves fissures in the heart's strongest steel. I have walked through flames that sought to consume, yet in their very midst, I learned the sacred art of endurance. Though I have been scorched, yet have I not shattered. Though I have stumbled, yet have I risen anew, bearing a love no longer fragile, but made enduring by the anvil of grief and the hammer of experience.

Thus do I turn now unto thee, Hephaestus, Lord of Fire, Smith of the Gods, Great Architect of all that endureth. Thou who wert cast from Olympus and yet raised marvels from the very ashes of thy fall — teach me thy craft. Instruct me in the forging of a love not borne of fleeting flame, but of embers that smoulder through the endless night.

Teach me to love in the silence where words falter; to give without diminishing; to endure alone if fate demand it, yet burn brightly with a steady, unwavering light. Let me not seek love in the careless blaze, but in the enduring fire that withstandeth storm and sorrow alike.

I crave not a love perfect in its beginnings, but one perfected by trial; not love that dazzles for a season, but love that remaineth steadfast when all else fades away.

Thus, unto thee, O Hephaestus, I raise this prayer:

O Hephaestus, Master of Flame and Iron,
Grant me a heart both fierce and untiring.
Let it be fashioned, not fickle nor frail,
But tempered by sorrow, steadfast to prevail.

May my love be not a spark that doth flee,
But an ember burning in eternity.

Teach my hands to build, and not destroy,
To forge a love no trial can alloy.

When the flames rise and the storms assail,
Let my resolve endure, let my spirit not fail.
Grant me a love wrought strong in the flame,
Unyielding, enduring, untouched by shame.

And when I give my heart, let it be known —
It is no passing fancy, but iron and stone.
A love hammered, forged, and purified,
A sacred fire that shall never be denied.

Chapter 12
The Messenger's Heart

When will you deliver the messages?

I have cast a thousand glances into the restless wind, each one a silent plea, each one a word left unsaid — yet none have landed where my heart had hoped. I grow tired of standing at life's endless crossroads, clutching letters that will never be read, prayers that will never be answered. I grow weary of sending love out into a world that refuses to turn its gaze back to me.

Love was never a race I sought to lose. It was a journey I began with reckless hope, a map hidden beneath my sleeve and a laugh tucked behind my lips. I was born not for waiting, but for chasing— to steal glances like a thief in moonlight, to gather fleeting moments and hoard them like treasures. I was swift, I was daring, I was foolish— much like you, O Hermes, Patron of Wanderers, Keeper of Secrets Unreturned.

Hermes, swift-footed and silver-tongued, I call upon thee. Take these words I dare not speak aloud; carry these confessions that no mortal ear will hear. Let my heart be your burden, and my longing your message, though I know it will fall into silence like all the rest.

They call me reckless, they call me wanderer— and they are not wrong. For I have learned that unreturned love does not favor the patient, nor the careful. It devours the bold and the desperate alike. Love is no gentle road, but a labyrinth of yearning, where every step leads farther from the one heart I seek.

I dance from heart to heart, not because I desire many, but because the one I truly wanted will not look back. I laugh because if I do not, I will weep. I run not to find someone else, but to outrun the ghost of a love I cannot bury. I live loudly because the silence of being unseen would otherwise destroy me.

Hermes, Guide of the Forsaken, Keeper of Roads and Forgotten Words, walk with me. Grant me cunning to survive the sting of indifference, swiftness to flee from memories that claw at my heels, and the courage to keep moving when the weight of unanswered love threatens to crush me.

Thus, I pray:

O Hermes, swift and sly,
Carry my sorrow through the sky.
Through twisted roads and endless sighs,
Deliver love that none replies.

Grant me wit to mask the ache,
A laughing smile I need to fake.
With winged heels, outrun regret,
And bury dreams I can't forget.

A trickster's grace, a fleeting glance,

Let me escape this hollow dance.
Not chained by hope, nor drowned by pain,
But moving onward through the rain.

O bearer of messages none return,
Steal me peace my heart may earn.
And may I find, through distant skies,
A place where unrequited love finally dies.

Chapter 13
Intoxicated

My view is spinning, yet still, my thoughts of her linger.

No matter how many times I drown myself in laughter, in wine, in a hundred distractions, it is still her— only her — who dances before my eyes like a fevered dream. I did not expect it to be thus. I believed love would be softer, gentler — something I might cradle neatly within the palm of my hand. Instead, it has swallowed me whole, torn through my carefully wrought defenses, and left me gasping for breath.

I stagger through this chaos, half-drunk on longing, terrified of how deeply I've fallen. There's no reason in me anymore, only raw, dizzying emotion. Love is my intoxication now — sweet, wild, and unstoppable. I laugh, I cry, I ache, I yearn — all at once, because loving her has turned me into a beautiful mess.

Dionysus, god of revelry and madness, you know what it's like to be lost in this fever. You who tear down walls with wine and ecstasy, show me how to survive this madness without losing myself completely. Teach me how to surrender to it, how to let this fever in my soul become a dance rather than a destruction.

Let my soul burn bright within this fire. Let my hands remain steady though the world spins ever faster. Let love be the wine that heals and wrecks me alike, and grant me the courage to drink it deep — without fear — until there remains nothing but the raw, terrible beauty of being alive.

Thus, I pray to you, O Dionysus:

Oh Dionysus, wild and free,
In this madness, carry me.
Let the wine blur right and wrong,
Let love be fever, fierce and strong.

Crown my hair with ivy green.
Steal my doubts, erase the seen.
Let my heart beat loud and wild,
A rebel's drum, a lover's child.

Flood my vains with sweet despair,
Tangle dreams within my hair.
Break me, make me, tear me down.
Cloak my sorrow in your crown.

Oh god of revel, song and flame,
Let love consume me without any shame.
And when I fall, drunk on this flight.
Let me be yours in endless nights.

Chapter 14
In the Quiet Hearth: The Heart Moves On

He was the home I no longer need to seek, for the place we built has ceased to belong to me. The door I once opened with ease is now closed, and the warmth we shared has faded into echoes of the past. I spent so long believing that love was something to hold onto, that the home we created would forever be my heart's resting place. But now, I understand — not all homes are meant to last, and some loves are not eternal.

Hestia, goddess of hearth and home, you know what it is to nurture something with care, to build from the ground up, and to feel the quiet ache when it all slips through your fingers. You understand the weight of giving love and the sorrow of watching it fade away. Letting go was never easy, but I've learned that holding onto what no longer fits is suffocating. So, with quiet acceptance, I let go.

The home he gave me, once a safe haven, has been abandoned, but I am not lost. I am still whole. And though I no longer seek refuge in the past, I carry with me the lessons of that home. Love isn't about possession or control; it's about knowing when to step away and allowing each soul the space to grow.

I will never forget what we shared, but I know now that it is time to walk away, to build a new home within myself. A home that does not rely on another, but one where I am both the maker and the keeper. The warmth of your wisdom, Hestia, has taught me that love can be both a place to return to and a space I create for myself.

O Hestia, goddess of hearth and peace,
In your flame, I find the calm I need.
Where once I burned in love's embrace,
Now I find a softer, steadier place.

You teach me strength to let go and grow,
To hold onto warmth without the sorrow below.
No longer bound by what once was,
I turn to you, the guiding cause.
Your flame endures, though love may fly,
In you, I build a home that never dies.

O Hestia, in your light I stand,
No longer needing another's hand.
I trust the peace you gently bring,
And in your hearth, my heart will sing.

Chapter 15
To Rise From the Depths

I find myself standing upon the precipice, caught between the world I once knew and the one I might yet create. I turn my thoughts to you, Persephone, Queen of Shadows and Spring's Resplendent Daughter, knowing that you, too, have walked the treacherous path between life and death, between light and dark. You, who emerged from the depths of the underworld, not unscathed, but transformed, blooming once again beneath the sun.

Is it truly possible to love after such betrayal? Can a heart, shattered by the cruelest of deceits, dare to trust again? I am unsure. Yet, as I consider your tale— of rising from the ashes, not as you once were, but stronger for the trials you endured— I wonder, perhaps there is hope still left for me.

The world around me has crumbled, and I, too, lie broken. But could it be, just perhaps, that within such wreckage, there is the possibility of renewal? A second chance for forgiveness, for peace? If you, Persephone, can hold dominion over both darkness and light, then perhaps, within me, too, there lies a way to forgive, not for the other, but for myself.

To entertain the thought of forgiveness is no easy task. It is a grievous weight to cast aside the bitterness, the anger, and the part of me that clings to pain as though it were a shield. Yet, in the quiet moments, I wonder:

could I, as you did, rise once more? Could my heart, too, find the courage to bloom anew?

I do not seek to reclaim the world as it once was, nor do I desire a love unmarred by scars. But I ask only for this — *a chance to be reborn, a chance to begin anew*. To cast aside the grief of the past and to embrace what might yet come. If you, Persephone, have risen from the shadow of death itself, then perhaps I, too, can find the strength to rise from the dark, and to trust, once again, in the possibility of love.

My Queen, I seek your guidance, and in humility, I offer this prayer:

Persephone, Queen of Night,
Guide me from darkness, bring forth the light.
Teach me to forgive, to set my heart free,
So that I may bloom as you once did, so bright and carefree.

In winter's cold, I've wandered too long,
Afraid to trust, afraid to be strong.
But now, like you, I seek the spring,
To rise again, and to hear joy's song.

Show me the way from sorrow's deep,
To a heart that no longer weeps.
Let me grow, not as I was,

But as I may be, with strength in my cause.

Guide me, O Lady, through shadows and strife,
To the warmth that awaits in the spring of life.
Let me rise from the ashes, reborn and new,
With forgiveness in my heart, and hope shining through.

About the Author

Midnightzky

Midnightzky is a writer from Bulacan, Philippines, who has been writing novels and poetry since she was twelve years old. Currently a Humanities and Social Sciences student, she draws inspiration from love, heartbreak, and the quiet moments often overlooked. Midnightzky is a campus journalist and a passionate storyteller who believes in the power of words to heal, awaken, and connect people. She writes across genres, blending reality and imagination to create worlds that feel both distant and familiar. When not writing, she enjoys reading, collecting books, and digital art. She shares her works online under the pen name Midnightzky on Wattpad.

www.ingramcontent.com/pod-product-compliance
Lightning Source LLC
LaVergne TN
LVHW041638070526
838199LV00052B/3442